P9-CCX-098

for Emma Sophia Price Olsen — W.A.

CIP Data is available.

Published in the United States 2003 by Dutton Children's Books,
a division of Penguin Putnam Books for Young Readers
345 Hudson Street, New York, New York 10014
www.penguinputnam.com

Originally published in Great Britain 2003 by Templar Publishing,
an imprint of The Templar Company plc, Surrey, Great Britain
Designed by Mike Jolley
Edited by Marcus Sedgwick

Printed in Belgium

First American Edition

ISBN 0-525-47114-6

2 4 6 8 10 9 7 5 3 1

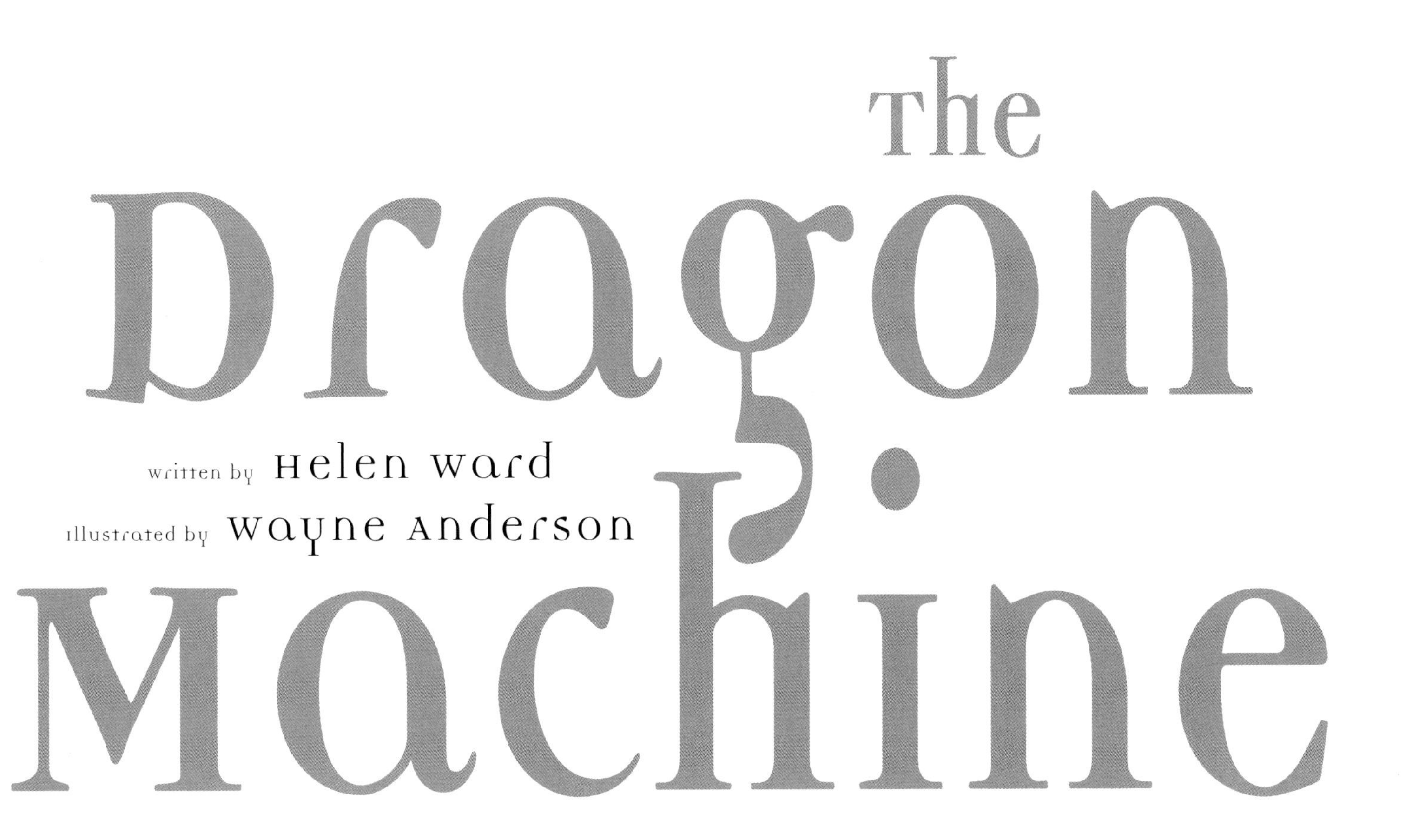

The Dragon Machine

written by Helen Ward

illustrated by Wayne Anderson

Dutton Children's Books
New York

George noticed his first
real dragon on a rainy Thursday.

And the more he looked, the more dragons he saw.

ignored and overlooked,
the dragons went unnoticed...

...just like George.

Dragons perched on the telephone wires

and lurked in the trash cans.

They chased butterflies through the tulips.

They teased the cat.

They sank the water lilies in the pond.

George fed them stale cookies and smelly cheese.

And that's
when the trouble began.

The dragons followed George everywhere.
George spent more and more of his time cleaning up muddy footprints and saying he was sorry for breaking things **he** had not broken.

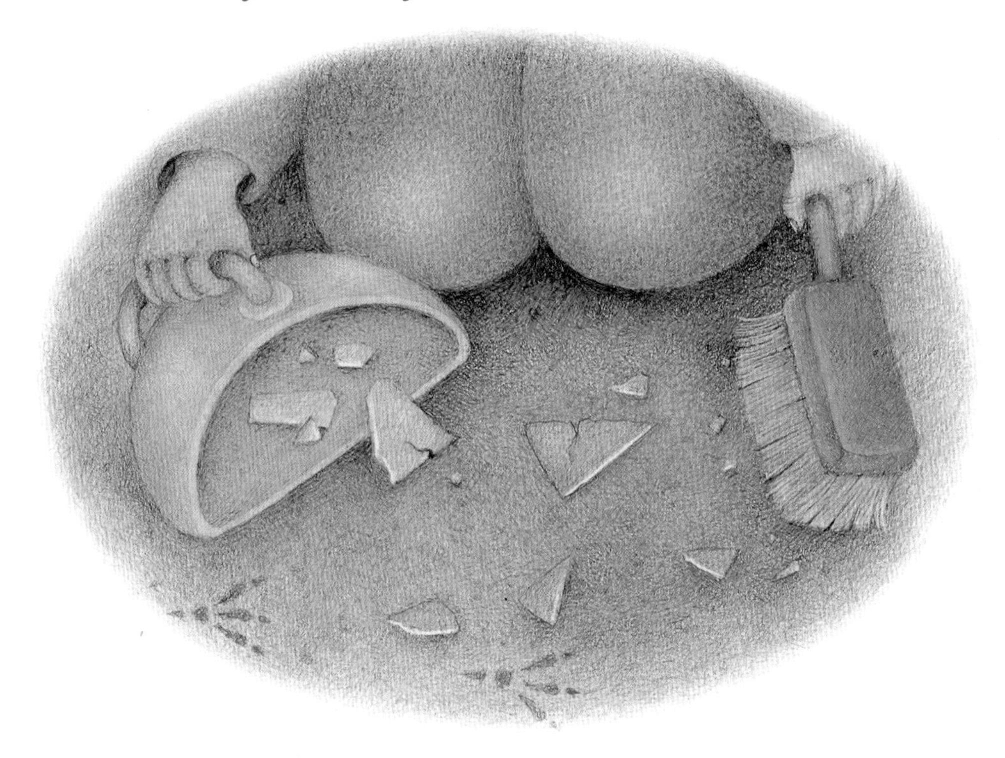

George's dragons were becoming too troublesome to stay unnoticed for much longer.

Something had to be done.
George went in search of some advice.

The dragons
followed George to the library.

He consulted **The Encyclopedia of Dragons.**
There were dire warnings: Never feed a dragon.
Never let a dragon into your home. Too late, thought
George. There were also tragic tales of dragons
discovered...and captured.

And then he found a map of the place
where dragons belonged.

It was a great wilderness, ignored
and overlooked and safe.
But George knew he would have
to show them the way.

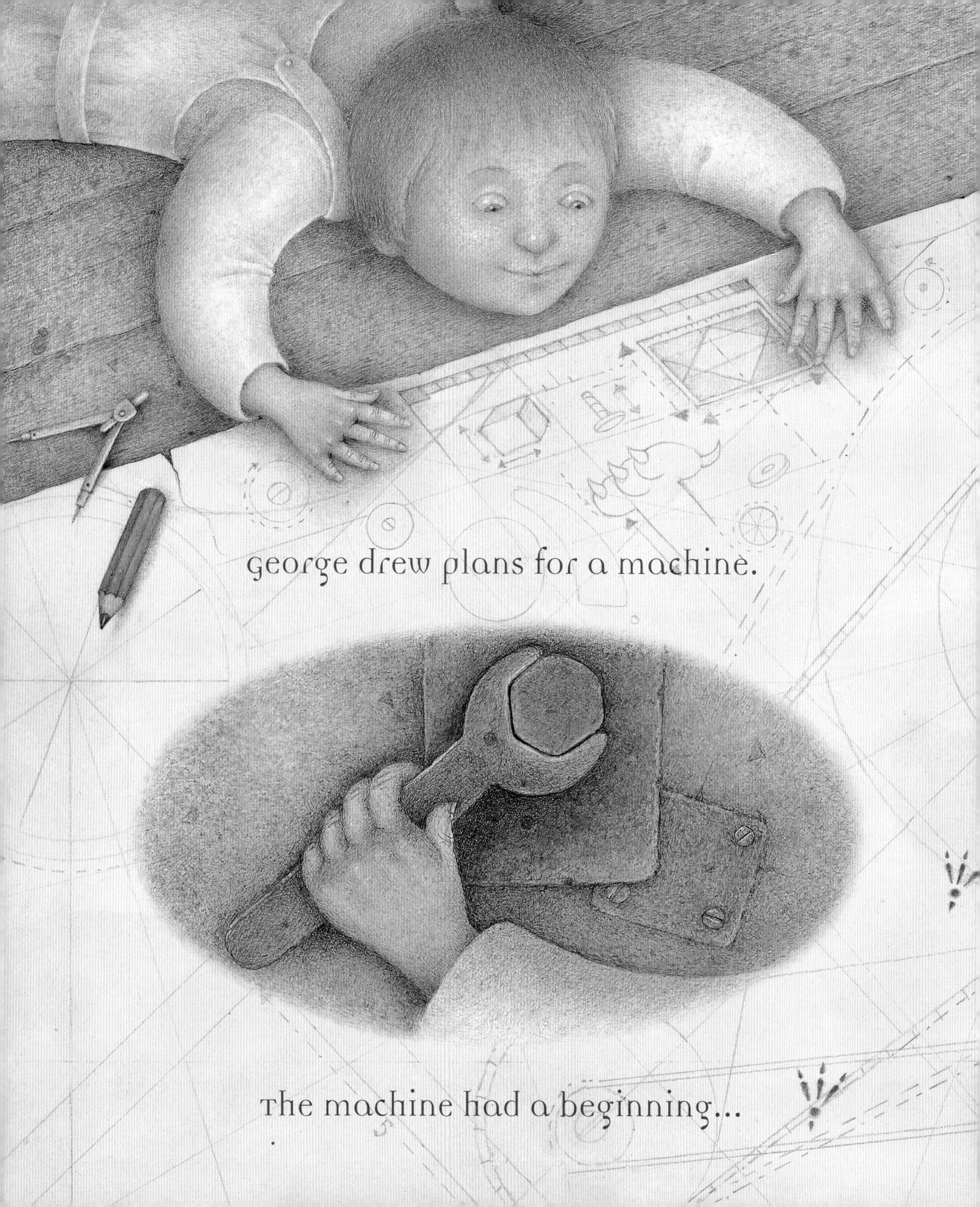

George drew plans for a machine.

The machine had a beginning...

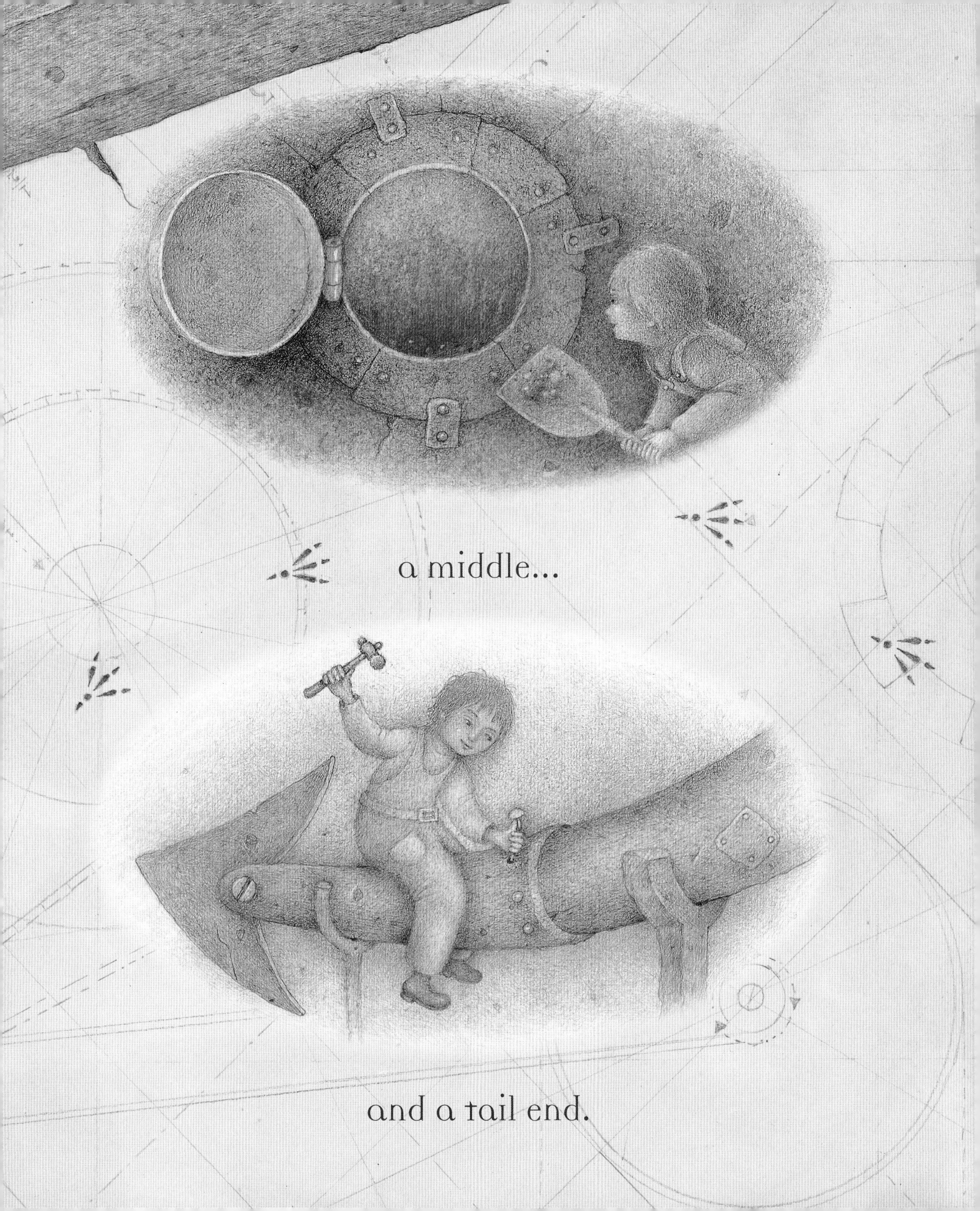

a middle...

and a tail end.

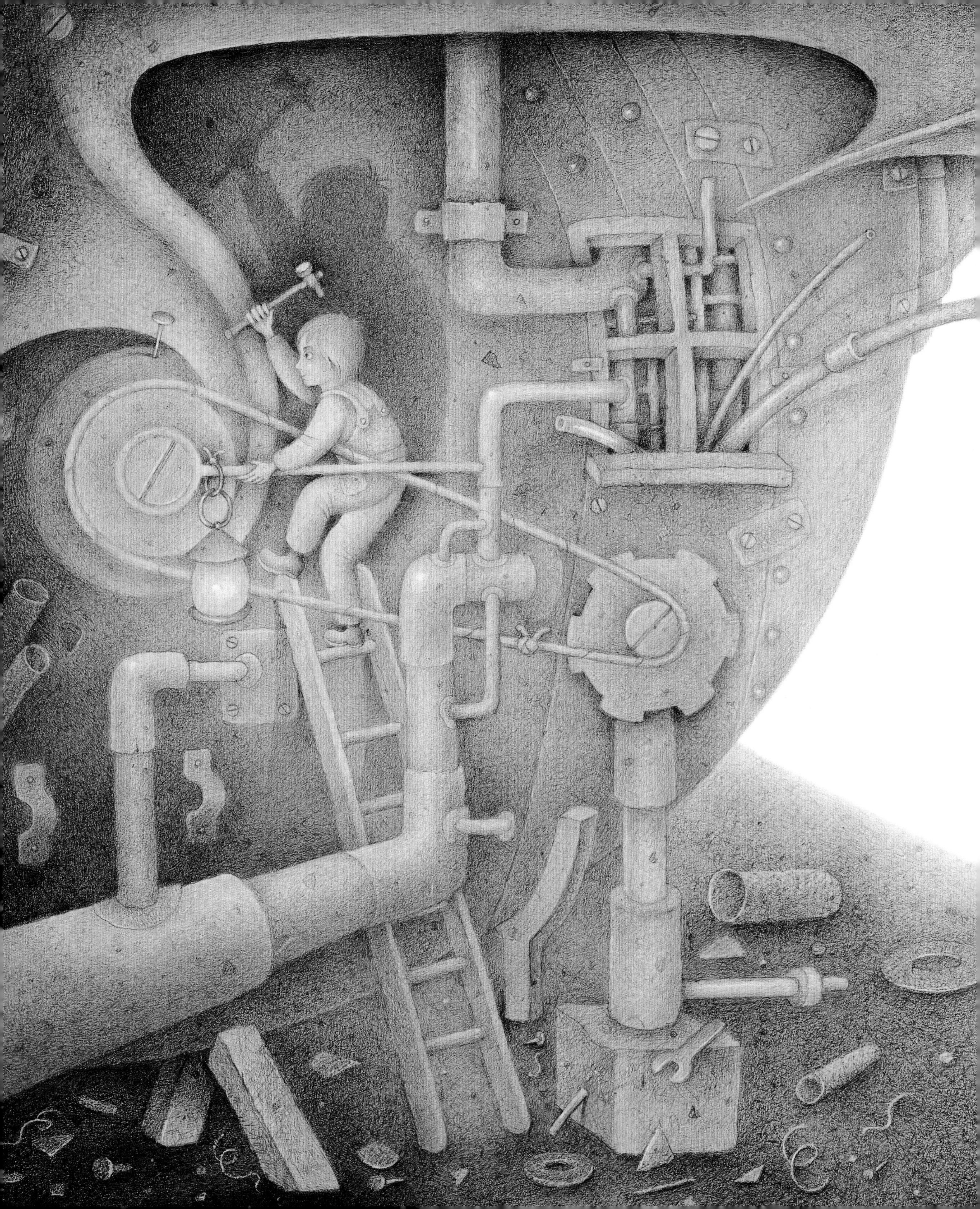

It had lots of pipes and pulleys
and beautiful, strong wings.

George hammered in the last nail.
He packed cookies and smelly cheese and
then climbed up into the cockpit.

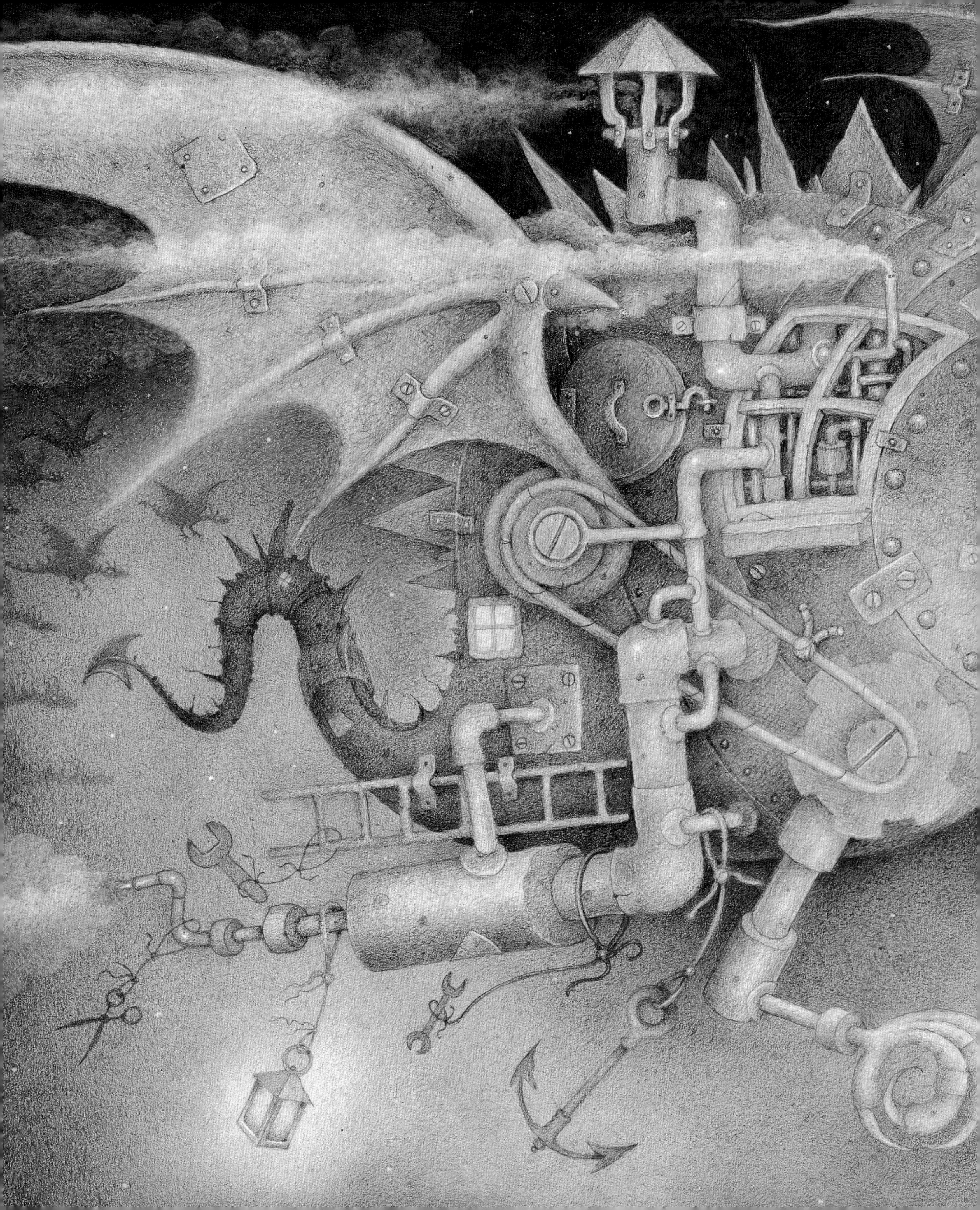

His dragon machine lumbered, engine ticking gently, into the night sky.

And the dragons followed.

The machine clicked
and whirred over the sleeping town.
It rattled and clunked
over the moonlit fields and woods.

The dragons followed.

It clattered and banged and blundered into the great wilderness with a crash.

The dragons followed.

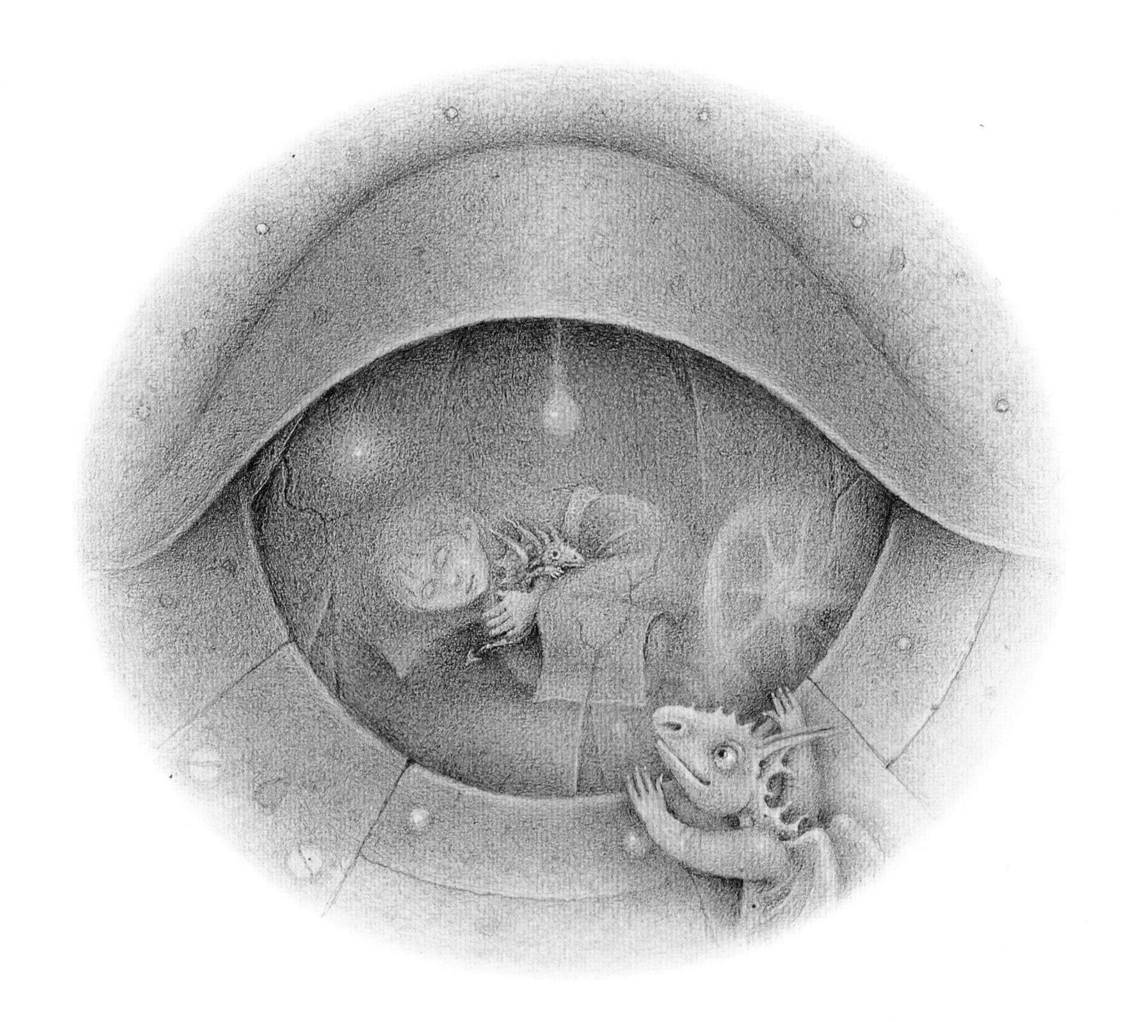

George was so tired from his journey that he fell asleep in the wreckage of his dragon machine.

By morning, all the dragons were gone.

There was an emptiness all around
and inside George...

...and an emptiness at home,
where George **should** have been.

His parents searched the town.
They searched the fields.
They ventured into the great wilderness,
looking for George, and found him among the
broken pieces of his dragon machine.

george and his dreams of dragons went home.

Everyone was happy to see George, and George was happy to be back. He was no longer ignored or overlooked.

His parents baked a huge cake to celebrate his return and even gave him a **dog** as a present. George was the only one who noticed there was something unusual about his dog...

...and George loved him
all the more.

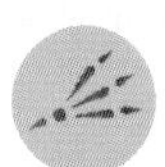